BBC CHILDREN'S BOOKS
UK | USA | Canada | Ireland | Australia
India | New Zealand | South Africa

BBC Children's Books are published by Puffin Books,
part of the Penguin Random House group of companies
whose addresses can be found at global.penguinrandomhouse.com.

www.penguin.co.uk
www.puffin.co.uk
www.ladybird.co.uk

Penguin
Random House
UK

First published 2020
001

Written by Paul Lang

Printed in Italy

A CIP catalogue record for this book is available from
the British Library

ISBN: 978–1–405–94607–0

All correspondence to: BBC Children's Books
Penguin Random House Children's
One Embassy Gardens, 8 Viaduct Gardens
London SW11 7BW

CONTENTS

MEET THE FAM

THE DOCTOR

FULL NAME: The Doctor

KNOWN ALIASES: The Doctor

OCCUPATION: Classified

Oh, it's you!

I was really hoping you'd be the one to pick up this book. I mean, don't get me wrong, everyone else is fine, but you – you're just a tiny bit special.

I'm a Time Lord. I travel through space and time in a blue box called the TARDIS, fighting monsters, defeating evil and keeping everything ticking over just nicely, thank you very much.

But every once in a while, I get locked up for a billion years or frozen in time or trapped in a parallel dimension where dogs are people and people are dogs . . . You know the sort of thing. And it's going to be down to you to protect Planet Earth from all the evil forces in the universe. No pressure.

That's why you need to read this book very carefully – so you're prepared. I'll be popping up all the way through with hints and tips, so look out for my special symbol. It looks like this:

You won't be on your own. I've got a whole gang on Earth who're ready and able to help. (Unless they're also stuck with me in the dog dimension, but hopefully that won't happen.) Seriously, have you seen these guys? They're amazing! Meet Team TARDIS . . .

GRAHAM

FULL NAME: Graham O'Brien

KNOWN ALIASES: Steve Jobs

OCCUPATION: Retired bus driver

HOME TOWN: Sheffield via Essex, Earth

YAZ

FULL NAME: Yasmin (Yaz) Khan

KNOWN ALIASES: Sofia Afzal

OCCUPATION: Police officer

HOME TOWN: Sheffield, Earth

RYAN

FULL NAME: Ryan Sinclair

KNOWN ALIASES: Logan Jackson

OCCUPATION: Warehouse worker

HOME TOWN: Sheffield, Earth

SPYFALL

THE DOCTOR'S DIARY

This was a busy old day. First up, we all got kidnapped by MI6 cos spies all over the world were having their DNA rewritten by something alien and nobody knew how to stop it.

I headed to Australia with Graham to find O, a struck-off secret agent living in the outback who had special knowledge of alien activities. Meanwhile, Yaz and Ryan went to California for a chat with Daniel Barton, a mega-rich tech genius whose company, VOR, held data on everyone in the entire world.

Barton turned out to be in league with the Kasaavin, alien light creatures who had broken through from another universe. Oh, and did I mention that O turned out to be the Master – a Time Lord, just like me?

Well, not much like me at all, actually – the exact opposite of me, more like it.

The Master lured me, Graham, Yaz and Ryan on board a private jet, which then exploded. We were facing certain death, but my gang landed the damaged plane safely. (Death's never totally certain when I'm around.)

Not that I was around – I'd been zapped into the Kasaavin realm, which was a whole lot of nothing. I got back with help from Ada Lovelace, to Paris in 1943, where we met super spy Noor Inayat Khan. What can I say? Brilliant gangs of brilliant people just seem to form around me! It's like my superpower. Well, that and flying, but I don't do that often as it's showing off a bit.

Speaking of show-offs,

I also caught up with the Master, who had teamed up with Barton.

But they hadn't counted on me and my new crew of coding experts! We'd seeded a fail-safe in computers throughout history. All I had to do was activate it to send the Kasaavin packing, back to their empty universe – and they took the Master with them. Bish-bash-bosh. Job done!

NEW FRIEND

C

Big boss of MI6, who summoned the Doctor to investigate attacks on the world's secret agents. He was assassinated by the Master. Poor old C.

NEW FOE
DANIEL BARTON

Double (possibly even triple) agent who once worked for MI6. Head of mega-tech company VOR. Barton teamed up with the Kasaavin and the Master to sell out humanity.

NEW TECH
LASER SHOES

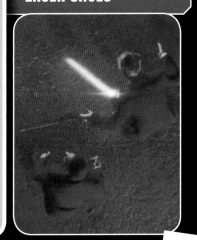

C kitted out the gang with loads of cool stuff, including Graham's fancy footwear! Graham's laser shoes shot out a bolt of energy every time he stamped his foot – very helpful when fighting off a pack of advancing Kasaavin! Shame he didn't know how to turn them off again. . .

HOW TO LAND A PLANE WITHOUT A COCKPIT

Find central walkway latch

Lift latch

Find cable

Plug into phone

I said hurry!

BE MORE DOCTOR

Don't forget to nip back in time to leave your fam the instructions they'll need when they get stuck on a crashing plane!

QUICK QUIZ

The Doctor visited Gallifrey to find it in ruins. But who destroyed everything?

A. The Daleks

B. The Master

C. The Kasaavin

ANSWER ON PAGE 61

THE KASAAVIN

Takes on the pattern of any surface it passes through

Crackles and howls when feasting

Body of pure light

Moves quickly

WHAT ARE THEY?
Violent and dangerous creatures from another dimension.

WHAT CAN THEY DO?
Phase through walls and rewrite human DNA.

WHAT DO THEY WANT?
To convert humans into living data-storage units.

WHAT ARE THEIR WEAKNESSES?
They're repelled by electrical force.

Leaves no scannable trace

Glitches under attack

TARDIS DATA EXTRACT
- Kasaavin can't consume time travellers – artron energy gives them indigestion!
- Kasaavin use physical contact to transport people in and out of their dimension.
- Sleeper agents are in place across every galaxy, preparing for conquest!

WARNING: Kasaavin are capable of breaching TARDIS defence systems. Emergency dematerialisation recommended.

WATCH OUT FOR . . .
Your phone or tablet – there could be a Kasaavin lurking in your apps!

CRACK
NOOR'S CODE

MORSE CODE

•—	A
—•••	B
—•—•	C
—••	D
•	E
••—•	F
——•	G
••••	H
••	I
•———	J
—•—	K
•—••	L
——	M
—•	N
———	O
•——•	P
——•—	Q
•—•	R
•••	S
—	T
••—	U
•••—	V
•——	W
—••—	X
—•——	Y
——••	Z

CODE NAME MADELEINE CALLING.

THIS MESSAGE IS OF VITAL IMPORTANCE.

PLEASE TRANSLATE URGENTLY.

Use the Morse code key to work out Noor's message.

```
— — —   • • — •   • • — •   • •   — • — •   •   • — •

— — —   • •   • • •   • —

— • •   — — —   • • —   — • • •   • — • •   •

• —   — — •   •   — •   —   /

— • • •   •   • — —   • —   • — •   •   /

• • • •   •       • •   • • •

— •   — — —   —   • — —   • • • •   — — —

• • • •   •       • • •   •   •   — —   • • •
```

ANSWERS ON PAGE 61

THE DOCTOR VS THE MASTER
THE BEST OF ENEMIES

By ME, the Master. Checked for accuracy by me, the Doctor.

I knew this psychic link was a bad idea.
And you might want to double-check some of
what you *think* is accurate, Doctor . . .

What's that supposed to mean?

You'll find out — and soon.
But enough about you — this is the story
of *my* life. Now, where to begin?

We used to be friends, and sometimes I forget exactly
how and why that changed. Why don't you start there?

And how exactly do *you* recall our early years, Doctor?

Two little children starting their journey to becoming Time Lords, staring into the abyss of the
Untempered Schism on Gallifrey. It was always said one of three things would happen to the novices:
they'd be inspired, they'd run away or they'd go mad.

I looked into the Time Vortex and saw the raw power of it.
But it changed me. Left a constant rhythm in my head.
The sound of drums. Driving me on . . .

Then you legged it from Gallifrey, just like I did. But I didn't
see you for ages after that. What were you up to?

My whole life doesn't revolve around you, despite what you *seem* to think, Doctor. Anyway, you seemed
happy enough when you did see me. Caught by the Time Lords and exiled on your wretched Planet Earth.
You were bored! You needed me to liven up your miserable life. You even took a job!

Oi, watch it. I loved that little job! Scientific advisor to the United
Nations Intelligence Taskforce. Sounds quite posh, doesn't it?

As usual, you chose to squander your intellect and power
for the benefit of lesser beings. But I took a different path.
I formed alliances, made plans, got things done . . .

Oh, yes, your 'alliances'! They didn't always work out though, did they? You'd go into business with
any alien who had half a plan to conquer humanity, without doing the most basic of
background checks. Remember the Axons? They did you up like a kipper, mate!

There were . . . challenges, I admit. But at least I was being proactive. I would have been triumphant eventually, if my physical form hadn't started to degrade.

And we all know what your solution for that was – stealing bodies! You're still doing that now. Remember what you did to the real O?

My need was greater than theirs, Doctor. And the Time Lords didn't seem worried about where my bodies had come from when they needed me to fight in the Time War.

You sneaked out of that one as well, thanks to the Chameleon Arch – disguising yourself as a human so you'd survive oblivion.

And, as usual, you blundered in and caused my true self to re-emerge. Not one of your best moves — especially when I then enslaved Earth and decimated the population.

Ah, but I reversed that! Didn't keep you down for long. You looked quite different the next time I saw you. I quite liked you as Missy. At least she wanted to change, to be a better person.

She spent too long in your company, Doctor — a mistake I don't intend to repeat. Don't forget: everything you know is a lie.

You keep saying that, so why don't you just come out and tell me what you mean?

Where's the fun in that? I'll tell you everything when I'm good and ready, and not one minute sooner . . .

PAST MASTERS

MY BEST ENEMY'S OLD FACES.

When I was trapped on Earth, the Master made my life hell. He was an old charmer when he looked like this – still evil, though.

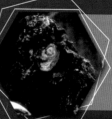

This is what happened when the Master tried to regenerate one time too many.

After stealing someone else's body, the Master was back in business.

Would you trust this face? Plenty did – he was elected Prime Minister of the UK!

Don't be fooled by the Mary Poppins look. Missy was every bit as dangerous as her other incarnations.

RYAN'S DIARY

You reckon travelling with the Doctor is one long holiday? You've gotta be kidding me! Tranquility Spa, they called it. I promise I've never been anywhere less tranquil my whole life – and I've been to actual battlefields.

I should have known how things were gonna go when I caught the Hopper virus off a vending machine at the hotel. I only wanted a packet of cheese-and-onion crisps, but I ended up getting electrocuted and losing the use of my legs.

That's when I met her, down on the floor. Bella. Proper beautiful, and she had the Hopper virus too, so we already had loads in common. She told me she was a hotel critic, which turned out to be a massive lie, but I told her I was a surgeon for pilots so I'm not really in a position to criticise.

The hotel was under this giant dome on a planet that was crazy wild – and I'm not just talking about the landscape. There were creatures called Dregs – they wiped out loads of the guests, but a few of us managed to get away.

This woman, Kane, was running the place. She was a shady character. She'd devoted her life to building the resort on an orphan planet – a planet so wrecked nobody is supposed to go there.

And Bella? She wasn't just on holiday. She was Kane's daughter, and she was pretty sore about being abandoned by her own mum. And by 'pretty sore', I mean 'blew the place up with a giant bomb'.

So, we were running out of oxygen and there was too much carbon dioxide in the atmosphere, but eventually we all managed to dodge the Dregs and fix the teleport cube. Bella even made up with her mum. But there wasn't enough power for everyone to beam off in one go. I got away, but I'm never gonna know if Bella escaped, too.

Oh, and the Dregs? It turned out that they were us – super-evolved humans from the future who'd mutated after destroying Earth. Living only to cause pain. That was a pretty bleak day. But I hope there's something we can do to change things. Something I can do . . .

Hoping to create a better future for her daughter, Kane built Tranquility Spa, a 'fakation' ecosystem, on the ravaged planet Orphan 55. She eventually saw the error of her ways and helped Team TARDIS to escape.

NEW TECH
TELEPORT CUBE

When Graham put together the six *Bandohzi Herald* coupons he'd collected to claim a free holiday, he activated a teleport cube. Graham, the Doctor, Yaz and Ryan were zapped across the galaxy four seconds later!

QUICK QUIZ

What's the best way to stop Hopper-virus hallucinations?

- [ ] **A.** Suck your thumb
- [ ] **B.** Stand on one leg
- [ ] **C.** Do a cartwheel

BE MORE DOCTOR

Humans forget how powerful they are. You lot can alter the course of history – for good and for bad!

ANSWER ON PAGE 61

DREGS

WHAT ARE THEY?
Mutated human beings, transformed by global warming, radiation and toxic pollution.

WHAT CAN THEY DO?
Adapt to guns and inhospitable environments, run at up to fifteen miles per hour.

WHAT DO THEY WANT?
To defend their territory.

WHAT ARE THEIR WEAKNESSES?
Oxygen. They breathe out oxygen and inhale carbon dioxide.

Blinking black eyes

Large, fanged jaws

Primal, animalistic roar

Sinewy, muscular torso

Glistening skin

Claws can tear off armour plating

Lean, powerful legs

WATCH OUT FOR . . .
The sounds of Dregs roaring – that means they're communicating!

TARDIS DATA EXTRACT
- Tranquility Spa is surrounded by an ionic membrane that acts as a defensive shield.
- Dregs don't just kill on instinct – they enjoy it!
- They gather in underground nests and sleep standing upright with their eyes closed.

WARNING: In the event of a Dreg incursion, head straight for the linen cupboard!

ACTIVITY
COLOUR CHAMELEON

I love my TARDIS. It's the best blue box in the galaxy. But it's not supposed to be blue all the time! It's stuck like that because the chameleon circuit – the bit that makes it blend in wherever it lands – is broken. Luckily, I quite like it how it is, but I do sometimes wonder what it would look like with a different coat of paint.

That's where you come in. I want you to create an alien landscape, then colour in the TARDIS to match. (And no cheating – I don't want to see the TARDIS beside a sapphire lake or parked on the Azure Plains of the planet Cobalt 17.)

TARDIS TRIP REVIEWER

THE TARDIS IS AMAZING. BUT IT DOESN'T ALWAYS TAKE US TO THE BEST PLACES . . .

EVERYTHING IS COMPLETELY NORMAL. THIS IS JUST A DRILL. WHAT SCREAMS?

TRANQUILITY SPA

Review by HAMMERS1234

No complaints about the price of this trip. After all, I got it for free with six coupons out of the *Bandohzi Herald*, which is pretty fan-da-Bandohzi. Rules about wearing Speedos outside the pool area were a bit strict in my opinion. Lush rainforest views were great. Could have done without the murderous super-evolved Dregs killing everyone, but, on the other hand, the cocktails were lovely. So it's swings and roundabouts, really.

ATTRACTIONS

- Oxygen*
- Pool
- Sun-kissed terrace
- Steam room
- Licensed for weddings (if bride and groom survive long enough)

*Mon–Thu only

4/5

VILLA DIODATI, LAKE GENEVA, SWITZERLAND

Review by GothGirlMary1797

Repaired to Villa Diodati in search of relaxation and fine weather, and sadly found neither in abundance. The air was so fetid and heavy that we hardly dared cross the threshold. On the bright side, the unusual qualities of this particular villa made it seem very spacious, with never-ending staircases, vanishing walls and other such modern enhancements. We all had a splendid time with dancing and music, until our good cheer was spoiled by the arrival of a most unsavoury gentleman. This modern Prometheus was made of human parts, and, while quite frightful, he might prove to be inspirational for my writings . . .

ATTRACTIONS

- **Charming lake**
- **Pianoforte**
- **Roomy cellar**
- **Library stocked with curiosities**

2/5

GLOUCESTER

Review by Pol-Kon-Don-1

Ko Fro Lo Bo Fro Sho! To No Bo Ko Thro No! Po Mo Lo So No Kro Do!! Go Bo No Ho Wo Do Zo! O! Xo Quo Go Bo Ro To Jo Co Vo!

ATTRACTIONS

- **Perimeter enforcement field**
- **Guided tours (subject to cancellation)**
- **Gloucester Cathedral**
- **Beautiful lighthouse**

1/5

FIRST TIME IN GLOUCESTER? TRY MY GUIDED TOUR!

SHEFFIELD

Review by ΘΣ

I've always had a great time in Sheffield, ever since I first dropped in. Train services are perfectly timed, and there's lots of construction going on for anyone who's a fan of giant cranes. The Town Hall is definitely worth a look – check out the ancient burial site beneath it if you can. Oh, no, actually, on second thought, don't go anywhere near the ancient burial site beneath the Town Hall. Take care choosing a place to stay – the Robertson Luxury Hotel is absolutely crawling with spiders! People generally very friendly. Some are now like family to me. It'll be the trip of your dreams (if you like dreaming about monsters and scary tattooed immortals).

ATTRACTIONS

- **Good base for intergalactic travel**
- **Regular alien sightings**
- **Pop-up art installation of a blue box that appears randomly in different parts of town**

5/5

NIKOLA TESLA'S NIGHT OF TERROR

YAZ'S DIARY

History is so complicated, especially when you find yourself slap bang in the middle of it.

We were at Niagara Falls in 1903, chasing something weird. We're always chasing something weird, except for when something weird is chasing us. This time it was an Orb of Thassor, an ancient device used to spread information. But this one had been hacked and was being used for something else. Something dodgy. And Nikola Tesla (yup, the famous inventor) had got his hands on it before us.

Tesla took it back to his lab in New York, where he seemed to be very unpopular – especially with his rival inventor, Thomas Edison. Tesla realised the Orb could power his experiments, so he hooked it up. Bad move. One of the people who'd interfered with it appeared and zapped me and Tesla on to a spaceship hiding over the city.

The ship belonged to the Skithra, a pack of scavengers who go around nicking other people's technology because it's easier than developing their own. The Orb was tracking Tesla cos the Skithra needed someone to repair all their defective gear, but their mardy scorpion queen decided I was surplus to requirements.

Luckily, the Doctor beamed up just in time to zap us out of there, which didn't please the queen one bit. She threatened to destroy the planet if Tesla didn't hand himself over. The Doctor was having none of that, and she helped Tesla finish the massive generator he was working on, then used its tower to blast the ship.

I thought what Tesla did would change everything for him – his invention had saved the world, so he'd become rich and famous, right? Wrong! The Doctor said that one crazy night wouldn't change his life at all. It doesn't seem fair that nobody will ever know what he did.

NEW FRIEND
DOROTHY SKERRITT

Tesla's faithful assistant was fiercely protective of her boss, and she loved the challenge of a life devoted to achieving things that seemed impossible.

NEW FOE
BILL TALLOW

When the Skithra killed the real Bill Tallow, a plant worker at the Niagara generator, one of them imitated his form – then went on a killing spree at Edison's factory.

NEW TECH
ORB OF THASSOR

The Thassor were an ancient race of storytellers and inventors who built orbs to send out among the stars as a way to share their legacy.

BE MORE DOCTOR

Even if things look hopeless, don't give up while you can still do some good!

QUICK QUIZ

What did the Doctor use to make her explosive powder?

■ **A.** Zinc nitrate and ammonium

■ **B.** Ammonium nitrate and zinc

■ **C.** Nitro nine and zinc

ANSWER ON PAGE 61

THE SKITHRA

Bone horns

WHAT ARE THEY?
Vicious alien scavengers.

WHAT CAN THEY DO?
Project human form using perception filters, and shoot energy blasts from stingers.

Scavenged armour

WHAT DO THEY WANT?
To steal technology and to destroy what they don't need.

Humanoid torso and head

WHAT ARE THEIR WEAKNESSES?
If the queen is destroyed, all the other Skithra will die too.

Electric stinger

WATCH OUT FOR . . .
People with burning red eyes – they could be a cloaked Skithra!

TARDIS DATA EXTRACT

- Skithra can take on the appearance of humans they've killed.
- The Skithra flagship can be made invisible using cloaking technology.
- Skithra have no idea how to fix all the tech they steal, so they have to kidnap scientists.

WARNING: Skithra can use their sting energy even when they're disguised!

NIKOLA TESLA'S WORD SEARCH OF WONDER

Ladies, gentlemen and giant scorpion queens, I come to you today to seek investment in my latest feat of wonder and imagination! Nobody will ever forget the names of my greatest inventions. How many words connected to my work can you find concealed in this fiendishly difficult puzzle?

```
H  U  E  E  N  X  O  V  Q  S  Z  C  U  H  Q  A  L
P  B  F  W  L  R  W  T  W  R  W  Y  P  N  R  J  A
A  V  F  I  B  F  F  Y  C  G  D  A  A  H  L  Y  B
R  J  Y  R  A  V  T  I  T  Q  R  V  T  E  E  Y  E
G  W  L  E  O  R  Q  P  A  G  Q  I  I  C  V  L  J
W  N  C  L  A  D  A  M  W  S  K  L  V  X  E  F  B
O  X  N  E  D  U  V  O  A  S  G  G  P  C  B  W  U
D  C  E  S  C  E  T  A  D  R  N  Y  T  V  T  O  Z
A  B  D  S  C  I  A  K  I  D  S  R  M  O  Z  X  V
H  W  R  W  O  H  F  T  M  A  I  I  G  X  W  M  A
S  X  A  F  R  U  F  I  H  C  N  D  W  H  C  R  M
C  F  W  O  O  N  D  J  N  R  T  P  O  G  A  O  S
W  F  A  P  V  Q  A  R  H  H  A  O  J  G  B  S  A
W  R  A  D  I  O  L  P  T  V  E  Y  A  W  O  S  S
E  K  L  Q  R  P  S  U  I  O  M  I  I  C  R  A  L
B  U  K  W  K  G  E  D  B  Q  N  V  O  S  Z  H  D
G  E  N  E  R  A  T  O  R  N  F  X  J  U  P  T  Z
Q  O  A  Z  Y  A  R  T  A  U  T  O  M  A  T  O  N
```

- ☐ AUTOMATON
- ☐ DEATHRAY
- ☐ ELECTRIC
- ☐ GENERATOR
- ☐ LAB
- ☐ MARS
- ☐ NIAGARA
- ☐ ORB
- ☐ RADIO
- ☐ SHADOWGRAPH
- ☐ SKITHRA
- ☐ THASSOR
- ☐ TESLA
- ☐ WARDENCLYFFE
- ☐ WIRELESS

ANSWERS ON PAGE 61

THE DALEK SURVIVAL GUIDE

Reckon you're prepared for a Dalek invasion of Earth?
Think again! Here's five really important things you need to know.

1. DON'T UNDERESTIMATE IT!

Daleks have a protective casing that acts as a life-support system for the creature inside. If the casing is destroyed, the Dalek is capable of slithering off and starting work on a new casing using any leftover bits. And you can't stop the mutant by, say, chopping it into three pieces and burying the bits at opposite corners of the globe – because they will find each other again.

2. WATCH YOUR BACK!

If a Dalek mutant finds itself without a shell, it might just decide to hitch a ride on you! A Dalek can wire itself up to a human brain by inserting a tentacle into the human's spine – eeewww! If your mate's started wearing a suspiciously big coat, check underneath it to make sure they haven't turned into a Dalek puppet.

3. FORGET THE STAIRS!

Don't listen to anyone who tells you that the best way to escape a Dalek is to head up the nearest flight of stairs – Daleks can levitate and even fly! You can buy yourself some time to escape by damaging the Dalek's eyestalk – but, even then, you'll have to be quick!

4. GET SMART!

Reckon you can raise an army to stop a Dalek invasion? You'll have to be cleverer than that. A single Dalek has enough firepower to destroy an entire army unit. In fact, just one Dalek at full power will eventually wipe out a whole planet! And, if it manages to summon the invasion fleet, you'll be done for in 9,376 rels!

5. CLEAN UP!

In the very unlikely event that you do manage to defeat a Dalek, make sure you clean up thoroughly afterwards. If even the tiniest speck of a Dalek remains, new Daleks can be grown! Your best plan is to launch the lot into a supernova – if you can get close enough.

THE RECONNAISSANCE DALEK //////////////

ights flash when talking

Eyestalk sends visual data to the brain

Improvised casing

Energy weapon from original shell

Grabber tool

Sensor globes

WATCH OUT FOR . . .
Ultraviolet light – it can revive an inactive mutant!

Red brain

Wriggling tentacles strong enough to overpower a human

WHAT IS IT?
One of the first reconnaissance scout Daleks to leave the Dalek home planet, Skaro.

WHAT CAN IT DO?
The mutant can restore itself if damaged or separated. It can also build a new shell from memory.

WHAT DOES IT WANT?
To gather information about Earth to send back home in preparation for an invasion.

WHAT ARE ITS WEAKNESSES?
This patched-up Dalek's weakened shell can be melted by microwaves.

TARDIS DATA EXTRACT
- This Recon Scout Dalek originally came to Earth in the ninth century.
- It was defeated by humans after an epic battle. They burned its shell and cut the mutant into pieces!
- One piece was left in Sheffield and accidentally revived, starting a deadly chain of events.

WARNING: This Dalek might look low-tech, but it's just as deadly as all the others!

FUGITIVE
OF THE JUDOON

THE DOCTOR'S DIARY

When you live the life I do, you're never quite sure what the day might bring. But nothing could ever have prepared me for what happened on this ordinary day in that ordinary town.

I was tracking a Judoon signal, and that's often the first sign of big trouble. They call themselves space police but they're more like mercenaries – they'll take any job and do anything to secure payment. And they'd placed a zonal enforcement field on Earth, which they're absolutely not allowed to do, but it meant that whoever they were looking for was on Earth. In Gloucester, of all places!

They did their usual thing of scanning for alien life forms, and this bloke called Lee Clayton seemed very keen to avoid them and do a runner with his wife, Ruth. But it turned out that he was protecting her. Only thing was, she had no idea why. As far as she was concerned, she was just a normal middle-aged tour guide with a normal middle-aged husband.

Lee sacrificed his life to save Ruth, and I helped her get to a safe place: the lighthouse where she grew up and where her parents were buried. But once we got there, everything started to come back to her. And there was nothing normal about Ruth whatsoever. She was actually me!

So how come I didn't remember her, and she didn't remember me?

It was actually a TARDIS buried at the lighthouse, not Ruth's parents, and it was soon in the grip of a Judoon tractor beam, with us inside. The Judoon had been hired by a woman called Gat, who said the other Doctor, Ruth, was a fugitive she was hunting for the glory of Gallifrey.

By then I didn't know what to think, but I wasn't getting any answers from Gat, as she was killed by a booby-trapped gun. The Judoon gave up and ran away, then the other Doctor just dumped me back on Earth. I had no answers and no idea what to do next.

And then, Graham, Yaz and Ryan told me they had a message for me – from Captain Jack Harkness. Just as I was trying to take all that in, the TARDIS alarm told me there was trouble on Earth. Gallifrey and the other Doctor would just have to wait . . .

NEW (OLD) FRIEND
CAPTAIN JACK HARKNESS

Graham woke up on the floor of a mysterious spaceship, and a man there, who – presuming Graham was the Doctor – gave him a big kiss! It was Captain Jack Harkness, an old friend of the Doctor's, and he had a **terrifying warning:** beware the lone Cyberman and don't give it what it wants – at all costs!

NEW FOE
GAT

This hard-as-nails Gallifreyan soldier set a platoon of Judoon the task of tracking down Ruth, who was on the run from her home planet. Sounds familiar . . .

NEW (OLD) TECH
THE CHAMELEON ARCH

This Time Lord invention allows the user to adopt a human disguise and avoid detection by anyone who might be in pursuit.

Make sure you have a thorough knowledge of intergalactic law so you can challenge any Judoon. And, if you don't, be really good at making up laws on the spot!

QUICK QUIZ

How do the Judoon mark a suspect they've eliminated from their enquiries?

- ☐ **A.** Implant a chip under their skin
- ☐ **B.** Stamp a big red X on their hand
- ☐ **C.** Add them to a database

ANSWER ON PAGE 61

THE JUDOON

Very cool hair

Sharp horns

Battle-scarred rhino face

Wrinkled grey skin

Large, powerful lungs

WHAT ARE THEY?
Intergalactic police
for hire.

WHAT CAN THEY DO?
Assimilate languages,
catalogue people, march.

WHAT DO THEY WANT?
To apprehend their
suspects and get paid.

WHAT ARE THEIR WEAKNESSES?
They're logical but not
very bright.

Strong, stocky build

Heavy leather military armour

WATCH OUT FOR . . .
Judoon temporal blasters –
they freeze time, and cause
massive damage and
radiation leaks.

TARDIS DATA EXTRACT
- They will operate outside their official
  jurisdiction – for the right price.
- Judoon are happy to issue compensation for
  any property they damage or destroy.
- A platoon of Judoon will happily catalogue
  a whole planet to find just one fugitive.

WARNING: Do not assault a Judoon officer –
even the lightest of taps means instant death!

CATALOGUE THE CRIMINALS

Bo! No sho tro fo . . .

++—ACTIVATING TRANSLATOR. Language: Human—++

Fugitives are trying to evade capture by disguising themselves as Judoon and hiding in this platoon. Cloning machine is faulty and can only make pairs. Catalogue the pairs. The unique Judoon is the true captain.

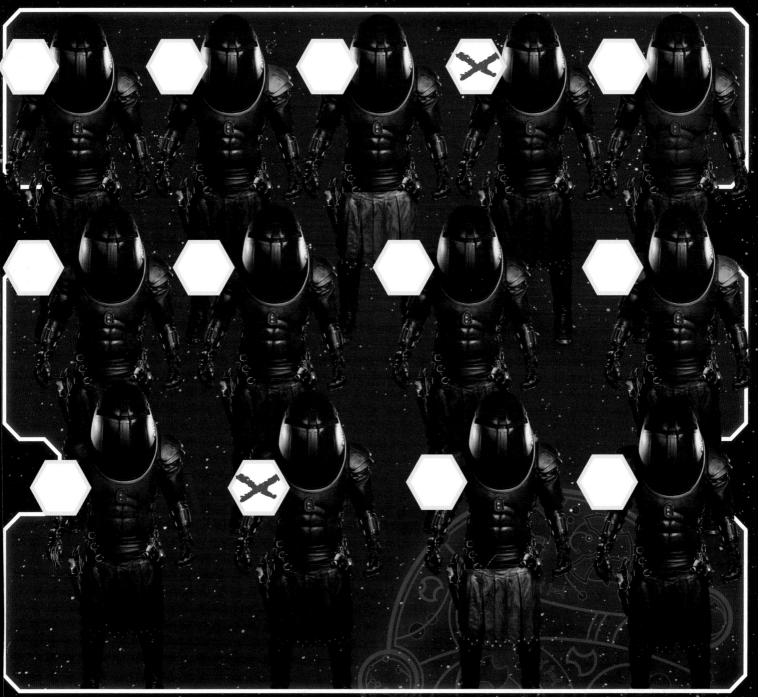

ANSWER ON PAGE 61

TOP FIVE CREATURES
WHO JUST WON'T QUIT!

The Doctor's always happy to see an old friend like me. But she could have lived without some of these creature comebacks . . .

1. DALEKS

When the Doctor defeated these deadliest of enemies on their home planet, he had no idea they'd be back throughout his different lives!

CLASSIC COMEBACK

The Daleks nicked the Earth and drove it halfway across the universe as part of a plot to destroy all forms of life (except Daleks!).

2. CYBERMEN

Earth used to have a twin planet called Mondas, and things worked out differently for the people there. They upgraded themselves into Cybermen!

CLASSIC COMEBACK

A big gang of Cybermen piled into our universe from a parallel one and had a massive dust-up with the Daleks at Canary Wharf. Awesome!

3. JUDOON

A platoon of Judoon upon the Moon caused some serious aggravation for the Tenth Doctor!

CLASSIC COMEBACK

A different platoon of Judoon seized control of Gloucester. Okay, that doesn't rhyme, but it was still a pretty daring plan!

4. ZYGONS

These sneaky shapeshifters almost had the Fourth Doctor baffled when they crash-landed in Scotland – and they brought the baby Loch Ness Monster with them!

CLASSIC COMEBACK

When their home planet got blown up, the Zygons settled on Earth disguised as humans. Could there be one living on your street?

5. WEEPING ANGELS

The Doctor and his pal Martha got zapped into the past by one of these stone assassins. They feast on the energy of the days people will no longer live.

CLASSIC COMEBACK

The Weeping Angels headed to New York and turned the Statue of Liberty into a giant Angel!

JACK'S BACK!

GUESS WHAT? I'M IMMORTAL SO I KEEP BOUNCING BACK TOO . . .

The first time I died it stung a bit, as I didn't know my friend Rose Tyler would bring me back to life.

Most people wouldn't survive clinging on to the outside of the TARDIS as it tore through the Time Vortex. Me included! But I just came back to life at our destination.

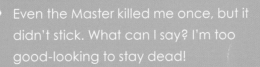

Even the Master killed me once, but it didn't stick. What can I say? I'm too good-looking to stay dead!

PRAXEUS

GRAHAM'S DIARY

The Doc was looking down in the dumps after that business with the Judoon and the other her. There's one thing that's always guaranteed to perk her up though, and that's the TARDIS getting a load of distress signals. Anything to distract her from what she's really thinking about.

These particular signals were coming from three different continents on Earth, so we ended up doing quite a bit of hopping about. And wouldn't you know it – the signals turned out to be connected! Nothing's ever a coincidence when the Doc's involved.

Yaz and I met this fella who was poking around a dodgy warehouse in Hong Kong, and we reckoned he had about as much right to be there as we did – so none at all. Meanwhile, the Doc was in Madagascar, investigating a missing US submarine. And Ryan? Well, poor Ryan was hanging out at a massive rubbish dump in Peru!

So, what was connecting these three places? You guessed it – people were dying. Birds, too. And all as a result of the same thing – these horrible white plastic tendrils that spread across their skin. The bloke Yaz and I had met, Jake, was trying to find his husband, Adam, an astronaut who'd been missing since crash-landing back on Earth. We tracked him down in the warehouse, only he was infected with the plastic whatsit as well. As for Ryan, he'd teamed up with Gabriela, a vlogger whose mate had been killed. No, I don't have a clue what a vlogger actually is either, mate.

Anyway, we all ended up in Madagascar, where a scientist called Suki helped the Doctor work out that the infection was attracted to all the microscopic bits of plastic that humans eat. The truth was a bit more complicated than that, though – Suki was an alien from a planet where this alien bacteria, Praxeus, had killed everyone, and she'd introduced it on Earth to help find a cure.

Unfortunately for Suki, the Praxeus got her before she could find her cure – but the Doc found one that worked on Adam, so that was Jake's cue to fly into space and spread the cure across the entire planet. Nice one, fella! The Doc says the planet's rid of Praxeus now, but we've still got serious plastic-pollution problems. It's never quite a happy ending, is it?

NEW FRIEND
GABRIELA CAMARA

A travel vlogger Ryan met in Peru. With her friend Jamila, she hosted the channel Two Girls Roaming – until they accidentally pitched up next to a rubbish dump and poor Jamila was scratched by a bird infected with Praxeus.

NEW FOE
SUKI CHENG

The Doctor trusted Suki because she was a scientist, but Suki had actually brought Praxeus to Earth, taking advantage of the planet's plastic problem to save her own race.

NEW TECH
LASER RIFLE

These nasty weapons were used by the hazmat-suited survivors of Suki's crew to defend their lab in Hong Kong.

BE MORE DOCTOR

Don't automatically trust someone because they do a job you admire — always work out what they're really about first!

QUICK QUIZ

How did Praxeus start spreading around the world?

- [ ] **A.** It travelled in the air.
- [ ] **B.** It was injected into people.
- [ ] **C.** It was carried by infected birds.

ANSWER ON PAGE 61

PRAXEUS CREATURES

Hazmat suit with breathing apparatus

Humanoid alien occupant

Plastic tendrils spread rapidly across body

Mutation is slower in some species

WHAT ARE THEY?

Living creatures infected with alien bacteria.

WHAT DO THEY LOOK LIKE?

Humans, except for the white tendrils that spread over the skin of the infected.

WHAT CAN THEY DO?

Spread the Praxeus bacteria on contact.

WHAT DO THEY WANT?

Nothing – carriers are just innocent victims.

WHAT ARE THEIR WEAKNESSES?

The bacteria eventually cause the carrier to disintegrate.

WATCH OUT FOR . . .
Microplastics in the body – the virus feasts on them!

TARDIS DATA EXTRACT

- The Praxeus bacteria spread outwards from the point of contact on an infected body.
- People killed by Praxeus might look like they're still moving, but it's actually just spasms caused by the bacteria.
- If a victim is wearing anything plastic, the parasite can fuse the plastic to the victim's body.

WARNING: Praxeus is attracted to all plastic – avoid areas of high plastic concentration!

PRAXEUS SOURCE

Make your way through all the plastic to reach the crashed spaceship. Avoid the Praxeus creatures and infected birds!

START

ANSWER ON PAGE 61

FINISH

TARDIS TOUR

Welcome to my TARDIS! It's so amazing – and it's always changing! Here's some of the coolest stuff to look out for . . .

THE CONSOLE
That six-sided thing in the middle is where all the action happens. I control the whole shebang from there. It's got six sides cos it originally had six pilots, but there's just me now.

SMOKE SCREEN
Some people have boring old monitors to keep an eye on stuff, but not me!

BIGGER ON THE INSIDE
Oh, I love watching people's faces when they walk inside for the first time. Tiny box on the outside; massive ship inside. I could tell you how it works but your brain would have to be bigger on the inside, too.

WHAT'S THE BOX?
The outside is based on one of those old-fashioned police boxes, which had phones that police officers used before they had radios or mobile phones. It's supposed to be able to change so that it matches wherever it lands, but the chameleon circuit broke a long time ago.

POLICE PUBLIC CALL BOX

POLICE TELEPHONE
FREE FOR
USE OF PUBLIC
ADVICE & ASSISTANCE
OBTAINABLE IMMEDIATELY
OFFICERS & CARS
RESPOND TO
URGENT CALLS
PULL TO OPEN

RIGHT ON TIME

As it's a time machine, I can steer the TARDIS to any point in history. Give or take seventy-seven minutes. Sorry, Yaz.

DIRECT INTERFACE

If I'm in a hurry, I can hook someone up to the TARDIS's telepathic circuits. It used to be easier when they were just a big bowl of goo, but now I need a special helmet and all sorts. Sometimes it gets a bit sparky.

OPEN-DOORS DAY

Now I think about it, inviting one of history's greatest inventors to have a nosy inside the TARDIS probably wasn't my smartest idea. Maybe if he figures it all out he can explain some of it to me. I've forgotten a few things over the centuries!

WORKING SPACE

I don't know about you, but when I'm making stuff I like to get absolutely everything I might possibly need and spread it all out on a big table so I can see exactly what I'm doing.

ONE OF A KIND?

You probably thought my TARDIS was unique, but there are some other Gallifreyan timeships knocking around. They're definitely not as good as mine, though.

THE MASTER'S TARDIS

When the Master turned up in the Australian outback, his house was actually a TARDIS. Then he vanished, so now I've got a spare. Handy, eh?

RUTH'S TARDIS

Pretty much like mine used to be back in the day – all gleaming, white and new. Mine's a bit more lived-in these days.

CAN YOU HEAR ME?

YAZ'S DIARY

Travelling through time and space is incredible, but sometimes it's nice to come home again. I had an important date with my sister, Sonya, while Ryan wanted to catch up with his mate, Tibo, and Graham had an urgent game of dominoes or whatever it is he does with his cronies at the bus garage, so the Doctor dropped us all back in Sheffield.

Dunno what she does when we all take time out. Ryan reckons she just zips ahead to when she's arranged to pick us up. Not this time. She took a trip to a hospital in Aleppo, Syria in 1380, where she met Tahira, who'd been terrorised by these horrible creatures.

Meanwhile, Ryan realised that Tibo wasn't doing so well. He kept being visited by this weird bald guy in his dreams – and out of them.

Then I dozed off and saw the same guy! Weird. Graham was having visions too, but, typical Graham, he was seeing something completely different: two worlds colliding and a woman calling for help. She was trapped between the planets in an orb thing, which was just managing to hold them apart.

Obviously there was a connection. The bald guy, Zellin, got his kicks from interfering with people's nightmares. He could even use them to make creatures like the Chagaska, the nightmares Tahira dreamt up. The Doctor thought Zellin had imprisoned the woman in the orb, so she set her free – big mistake! The woman was called Rakaya, and Zellin was on her side, feeding her the nightmares he collected.

With Rakaya loose, the pair headed to Sheffield to cause chaos, but the Doctor managed to summon them to Aleppo. Zellin's party trick was to detach his fingers and send them off to draw people's nightmares out through their ears, but the Doctor turned the tables on him. She sent a couple of stray fingers into Zellin's own lugholes, condemning him and Rakaya to their nightmare fate: being trapped together in the orb with a load of Chagaska. Back in your box, immortals!

Once it was all over, Ryan started to feel dead guilty about not being there for Tibo and his other mates. Travelling with the Doctor is everything I ever wanted, but I'm starting to wonder if it's the same for him . . .

NEW FRIEND
TAHIRA

A patient at Bimaristan Arghun Al-Kamili, an early psychiatric hospital in Aleppo, who's plagued by visions of terrifying creatures from her imagination – which soon become only too real!

NEW FOE
ZELLIN AND RAKAYA

Immortals who descended from a higher realm. They set two planets to war after betting on who could bring a planet to destruction first. But the people on the planets trapped Rakaya, the more powerful of the pair, in a prison orb.

NEW TECH
FREAKY FINGERS

Zellin could remove his fingers and send the detached digits scuttling into the ears of his victims to suck out their dreams. He also used them as flying attack weapons!

BE MORE DOCTOR

Never trust an immortal. Trust me.

QUICK QUIZ

Who haunted Graham
in his nightmare?

- ☐ **A.** Grace, his late wife
- ☐ **B.** The Doctor
- ☐ **C.** Ryan

ANSWER ON PAGE 61

THE CHAGASKA

Strong sense of smell

Lots of teeth on extra jaws

Long limbs

More than 8 feet tall on hind legs

Clawed hand

WHAT ARE THEY?
Creatures of Tahira's imagination, brought to life by Zellin.

WHAT CAN THEY DO?
Hunt down human prey – even though they technically don't exist!

WHAT DO THEY WANT?
Nothing. They don't have a consciousness of their own.

WHAT ARE THEIR WEAKNESSES?
They can't attack their creator, Tahira.

WATCH OUT FOR . . .
Empty rooms. Take a quick look up, just in case there's a Chagaska hanging from the ceiling!

TARDIS DATA EXTRACT
- Chagaska like it when their prey puts up a struggle!
- Chagaska fur doesn't register at all with the TARDIS scanners.
- Once Tahira knows the creatures come from her imagination, she's no longer afraid of them.

WARNING: The Chagaska might technically not exist, but they can still do you serious damage!

ZELLIN'S NIGHTMARE WORLD

After I visit your dreams, you may recall things differently from how you did before. There are seven differences between these two memories. Find them, or I will live in your nightmares forever . . .

Tick a box each time you find a difference

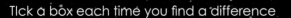

1	2	3	4	5	6	7
☐	☐	☐	☐	☐	☐	☐

THE HAUNTING OF VILLA DIODATI

RYAN'S DIARY

Our trip to Sheffield got pretty heavy, and I wasn't sure how I was feeling about . . . anything, really. But there's never much time to dwell on feelings in the TARDIS, so the Doctor whisked us straight off to Lake Geneva in Switzerland to meet Mary Shelley, on the night she had the idea for *Frankenstein*.

The summer of 1816 was harsh! Thunder, lightning, rain like I've never seen. We must have looked a state when Mary and her mates opened the door to us. She was still Mary Godwin then, but Percy Bysshe Shelley was already on the scene. (Although he wasn't in the house, which the Doctor thought was weird, as history said he was.) Lord Byron was there, with his girlfriend, Claire. At least, I think she was his girlfriend – the man had a bit of a wandering eye, which Claire wasn't happy about.

Then there was Dr Polidori, and he just looked knackered. Maybe I shouldn't have mentioned that though, since he challenged me to a duel with pistols.

I was wondering how I was gonna get out of that one, when this hand just full-on scurried across the room on its own. The duel was forgotten about pretty quickly after that, and things just got weirder and weirder: moving skeletons, stairs that you went down only to find yourself back at the top again, Polidori walking through walls . . . It was all going on.

Anyway, we soon found out where Mary got the idea for her book, cos a 100 per cent Frankenstein-y guy just appeared out of thin air. Got the Doctor really rattled, like it was something she'd seen before, but different. She called it a Cyberman, and

that's when the warning bells went off: a Cyberman was what Captain Jack had warned us about.

It was looking for the guardian of something it wanted, only nobody seemed to be guarding anything. Until we finally found Shelley. He'd found this liquid metal stuff, Cyberium, which was actually an artificial intelligence used in a future war. Someone had sent it back to change history, and the Cyberman wanted it – badly.

And the Doctor just . . . handed it over. We tried to talk her out of it, but she got really dark and told us she was the boss and we had to respect her decision, even if we didn't understand it. She said her next job was to head to that war in the future and stop the Cyberman. And did we follow? She's the Doctor – course we did!

NEW FRIEND
DR JOHN POLIDORI

Everyone was baffled when Polidori seemed to be sleepwalking through walls – until they realised there was a perception filter in the house, and he was the only one who couldn't see the fake walls it was throwing up.

NEW FOE
THE HAND

Ryan ended up on the wrong end of a disembodied hand. It had been reanimated by the power of the Cyberium, which was programmed to find spare human parts.

NEW TECH
CYBERIUM

This glimmering liquid metal moved like quicksilver, and was intelligent enough to control the strategy for a whole war.

BE MORE DOCTOR

They say you shouldn't put off until tomorrow what you can do today, but sometimes that's the exact opposite of what you need to do!

QUICK QUIZ

What was the name of Mary's baby?

- **A.** Frank
- **B.** William
- **C.** Ryan

ASHAD

Bloodshot eyes

Bad breath

Part of original face visible

Particle containment chamber

Metallic armour

Rougher and more primitive than usual for Cybermen

Metal bolted on to flesh

WHO IS HE?

A primitive, unfinished Cyberman.

WHAT CAN HE DO?

Lift a person with one hand, blast from an arm-mounted gun, detect vital signs.

WHAT DOES HE WANT?

To find the Guardian, retrieve the Cyberium and restore the Cyber empire.

WHAT ARE HIS WEAKNESSES?

He's unstable and still able to feel emotions.

WATCH OUT FOR . . .
Lightning! This creature can use it to recharge its own batteries.

TARDIS DATA EXTRACT

- This lone Cyberman travelled back through time from a devastating war in the future.
- Has a super-computer fused to its cerebral cortex.

WARNING: Beware the lone Cyberman! Do not give it what it wants!

MARY SHELLEY'S
MONSTROUS
MASH-UPS

I have witnessed many horrors in my life, but none so terrible as these creatures made of other creatures. Help these wretched souls return to their original forms.

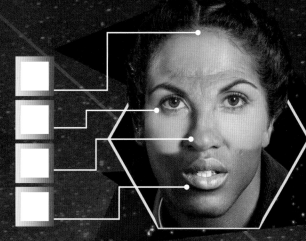

FAM

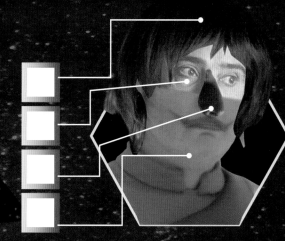

FRIENDS

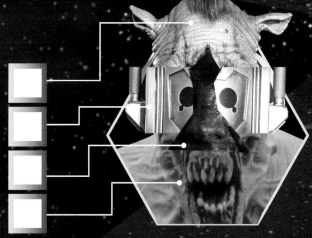

MONSTERS

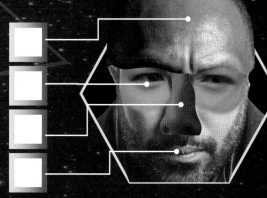

VILLAINS

INSTRUCTIONS

Each freaky face is made from bits of four different heads. Can you recognise everyone?

Write the numbers for each person or creature in the box next to their picture.

1. The Doctor

2. Hyph3n

3. Dreg

4. The Master

5. Suki

6. Nevi

7. Graham

8. The Skithra Queen

9. Gat

10. Captain Pol-Kon-Don

11. Yaz

12. Cyberman

13. Nikola Tesla

14. Daniel Barton

15. Lord Byron

16. Ryan

ANSWERS ON PAGE 61

HISTORY'S FINEST

We have met some cracking people from Earth's past on our travels with the Doc. Check out this incredible bunch . . .

ADA LOVELACE

Who was she?
A maths boffin who was crucial to the invention of the first computer.

When did she meet the Doctor?
In the Kasaavin realm. Ada had been snatched from 1834 and taken there. She returned with the Doctor to defeat the Kasaavin.

What happened to her after that?
She died in 1852 after many years of ill health. Her part in the development of computers wasn't discovered until a hundred years later!

NIKOLA TESLA

Who was he?
A brilliant inventor. Some of his original ideas inspired the invention of WiFi!

When did he meet the Doctor?
At Niagara Falls in 1903. He then travelled to New York City and, together with rival inventor Thomas Edison, assisted in the downfall of the Skithra, a race of scorpion-like scavengers.

What happened to him after that?
He carried on inventing, but sadly never achieved his true potential and he died penniless in 1943.

NOOR INAYAT KHAN

Who was she?
The first female wireless officer to be dropped behind enemy lines by the Allies during World War II. Her code-name was Madeleine.

When did she meet the Doctor?
Paris, 1943, after the Doctor and Ada Lovelace hid from the Master under her floorboards. Noor showed the Doctor how to send a fake message to the British claiming that the Master was a double agent.

What happened to her after that?
Noor was betrayed to the Nazis and arrested. She didn't live to see the end of the war.

MARY SHELLEY

Who was she?
The brilliant novelist who wrote *Frankenstein*, one of the most famous horror stories of all time. And her mate Lord Byron was Ada Lovelace's dad!

When did she meet the Doctor?
The Doctor wanted to take Ryan, Yaz and Graham to meet Mary on the night she had the idea for *Frankenstein*, in June 1816, but strange things were happening that didn't fit in with the established timeline – and there was a Cyberman on the loose!

What happened to her after that?
Mary became a widow aged twenty-four when her husband, Percy, drowned. She carried on writing to support herself. She died in 1851.

THE DOCTOR'S DIARY

When you've lived as long as I have, you tend to have a pretty good idea of who you are and what you stand for. But what happens when it turns out you've lived even longer than that, and it seems like you might be someone completely different?

I'll come back to that in a minute. Let's rewind a bit first, though . . .

I still had to track down the Cyberium, millions of years in the future. The Cyber Wars had been raging for a long time, and we found a small band of humans – the last survivors. We didn't have much to fight with, but we had to help. The Cybermen attacked, and we lost some of those surviving humans.

The Fam got separated – Yaz and Graham managed to get away on the humans' ship, while Ryan and I stole a Cybercarrier and headed for the Boundary – a mythical gateway to another dimension, and our only hope of reaching safety.

Yaz and Graham headed there too, but ended up on a massive Cybercarrier, full of thousands of new warriors, waiting to be revived. They might have been fine if the Cybermen had stayed dormant, but Ashad was also on board, and he soon got busy reviving his new army.

Meanwhile, Ryan and I reached the Boundary, where we met Ko Sharmus – an amazing man who'd been helping humans through the portal and out of harm's way. But, when it finally opened, I wasn't ready for what I saw on the other side: Gallifrey.

The Master jumped through the Boundary, then forced me to go back with him to the ruins of my old home. He couldn't wait to tell me why he'd destroyed the planet and killed everyone on it. And it was because of me. A secret about my past had made him completely flip out and destroy everyone and everything.

But the Master wasn't finished. He trapped my mind in the Matrix – a mega-storage drive full of Time Lord brains – then shrank Ashad to death and absorbed the Cyberium. Finally, he created the CyberMasters, a new race of hybrids that were part Cyberman, part Time Lord, with the ability to regenerate. Unstoppable warriors.

There was no way I could allow creatures like that to be loose in the universe, and I was left with only one choice: to use the Death Particle, which was still held in Ashad's shrunken armour, and destroy all biological life on the planet. But was that really something I could do? Of course not, but that didn't leave a lot of other options

Luckily, Ko Sharmus – who'd come through the Boundary too – appeared in the nick of time and told me to run while he activated the Particle. He was unbelievably brave, and without his noble sacrifice, the Cyber Masters could have wiped out all other living creatures, everywhere, all through time.

After all that, I just wanted to get back to Earth, where the Fam had gone in a spare TARDIS. That's gonna be easier said than done, though – I'm currently banged up in a Judoon prison, and I've been sentenced to life, which is rather a long time for me...

NEW FRIEND
RAVIO

One of the last remaining humans in the universe at the end of the Cyber Wars. She'd been a nurse but ended up as a refugee on a distant planet, desperately trying to reach the Boundary.

NEW FOE
CYBER DRONES

These war-battered Cyber heads fly in swarms and can take out equipment, buildings and people with laser bolts from their eyes.

NEW TECH
THE DEATH PARTICLE

A single particle created by the Cyberium with the power to destroy all organic life. Ashad held the Particle in the centre of his chest unit.

QUICK QUIZ

What are Cybermen thought to be allergic to?

- **A.** Gold
- **B.** Silver
- **C.** Bronze

ANSWER ON PAGE 61

BE MORE DOCTOR

Don't ever think nobody cares. That's simply not true – not as long as I'm still alive.

THE SECRET OF THE
TIMELESS CHILD

When you've lived as long as I have, you tend to have a pretty good idea of who you are. But what happens if you've actually lived even longer, and you might be someone completely different?

Once upon several times, before the Time Lords, there was an explorer. Her name was Tecteun, and she came from Gallifrey, a very ordinary planet that most of the universe had never even heard of. Tecteun was the first Gallifreyan to travel in space. She took risks to explore the worlds and galaxies beyond her home. And it was on one of these distant, deserted worlds at the far edge of another galaxy that she found something impossible. A gateway into another, unknown dimension.

Beneath it Tecteun found a child, abandoned and alone. She couldn't just leave the child, so she adopted her and the two set off on their travels together. Eventually, they returned to Gallifrey, where Tecteun studied the child for clues about where she might be from. But her secrets remained hidden.

Then, one day, there was a terrible accident. The child fell off a cliff and died. Tecteun thought she'd lost the child forever, but then something incredible happened. The child started to glow with a glittering, golden light. And she regenerated – the first person on Gallifrey ever to do so.

Tecteun became obsessed with studying the child, determined to crack the regeneration code. Eventually, she did. But, before she could share this incredible secret with her fellow Gallifreyans, Tecteun tested the theory on herself. The process worked, and Tecteun allowed others the power of regeneration – but there was a strict limit. Each Gallifreyan could only change twelve times. And that's how the Shobogans of Gallifrey became the Time Lords.

THE DOCTOR HAS BEEN THE DOCTOR FOR MUCH LONGER THAN SHE THOUGHT. AND ONE OF THE PEOPLE SHE USED TO BE WAS ME!

MEET THE DOCTOR

Where do I fit in to the Doctor's past? Was her memory erased? Did someone force her to become a child again?

I went into hiding to get away from Gallifrey, living my life believing I was a human called Ruth. But I was a fugitive – and someone had sent the Judoon to hunt me down.

Who wanted me so badly? And why was I so desperate to get away? These are all questions for the future. Or is it the past? You'll find out, one day . . .

THE CYBERMASTERS

Metal collar with Time Lord symbols

Completely flat face

Frowning mouth

Similar body to Cyberwarriors

Converted Time Lord body inside

Protective cloak with Gallifreyan designs

WHAT ARE THEY?
Time Lord corpses converted into Cybermen by the Master.

WHAT CAN THEY DO?
Everything a Cyberwarrior can, plus the ability to regenerate endlessly.

WHAT DO THEY WANT?
To become the dominant life-form in the universe.

WHAT ARE THEIR WEAKNESSES?
They are only vulnerable to a Death Particle, which would completely destroy the organic part.

WATCH OUT FOR . . .
The Death Particle! If you use it against the CyberMasters, you'll die too!

TARDIS DATA EXTRACT
- Ashad wanted to make the Cybermen fully robotic, but the Master killed him and switched to his own plan!
- When the Master killed all the other Time Lords, he kept them on ice to use later. Yuck!
- He used the bodies to create the CyberMasters – a fusion of Cyber and Time Lord tech, with an extra sprinkle of his own twisted imagination.

WARNING: The Master has full control over the CyberMasters, thanks to the Cyberium.

THE DARK TIMES
TIMES

There's one time period that even Time Lords don't visit. The Dark Times, right at the very dawn of the universe. So, what did I do? I visited! Several times. I looked a bit different from how you know me now, but you'll be used to other versions of me so I doubt you'll worry too much. I am a man, though. Bit weird, but I've been through worse . . .

By Melody Malone
Times Editor

THE TIME LORD VICTORIOUS?

🜨 Kotturuh battle crisis 🜨 Dalek Empire rises

The Kotturuh crisis has intensified following the Doctor's intervention (well, of course it has!), and Dalek involvement now threatens the fabric of the universe, according to the latest reports from the Dark Times.

Since the rise of the Kotturuh – the so-called 'Bringers of Death' – no species in the universe has been spared from their incredible power. And, after a period of immortality for all living creatures, the situation has changed dramatically.

The current crisis began when the Kotturuh discovered they had a terrible power: the ability to end or limit life. They see death as their religion and their gift – and they have been roaming the universe, doling it out.

Often the Kotturuh visit worlds peacefully and allocate lifespans after talking with the people who live there. But on other occasions, they appear in the skies and obliterate the population with no discussion.

Some have said that the Kotturuh's actions are necessary to prevent any one society from becoming too dominant, or to limit the spread of 'unworthy' species. Others have fought back or fled.

The arrival of the Doctor in the Dark Times has altered the course of the battle. Can he bring order to the chaos? Fat chance, but I'm sure he'll set the cat among the pigeons, at least. And how will the rise of the Dalek Empire affect the situation? Not favourably, I expect.

With the Doctor on the war-path, and on the run from his own death, the situation has never been more dangerous – or thrilling!

Hello, sweetie!

I'm Melody Malone, editor of the *Dark Times Times*. At least, that's my professional name as a journalist. You might know me better as River Song – time traveller, writer, archaeologist, explorer, detective, devoted wife, loving daughter and one of the most dangerous people who ever lived. All of which makes me uniquely qualified to tell you about one of the most dangerous times in the history of the universe. After all, there aren't many of us left who have visited . . .

My old man – my on–off husband and occasional wife, the Doctor – used to talk about the Dark Times. The times of chaos. The universe had only just formed, you see. There'd been a very Big Bang (I've

helped cause at least a few of those in my time) and everything came into being, all at once. Every planet, every species, every society, every flavour of frozen yoghurt – they all started with that event.

Everyone got along famously for a millennium or two, back when even the Eternals were young. But it didn't last. Because the Kotturuh were coming.

They were one of the very first species to explode into life, and it wasn't long before they revealed their party trick – death. This bunch were almost as fond of drama as I am.

Once they set out on their mission of death, there was no force or creature that could stop them, nor

was there any escape. Once a Kotturuh touched a species with death, it spread. Death might not come immediately (if you were lucky) but come it would.

The other established races were, understandably, rather peeved at these upstart Bringers of Death, and they reacted in different ways – some nobler than others.

If you're going to keep up with the terrifying tales of the Dark Times, you'll need to know something about the main players. Luckily, I stopped off on Gallifrey before it was destroyed and I managed to conceal the Black Scrolls of Rassilon upon my person, so the stories have survived . . .

The Kotturuh

What are they?

The Bringers of Death were one of the earliest species created by the Big Bang. They are immortal, but they also have the power to take death wherever they go.

What do they look like?

Very swish indeed. They wear gorgeous robes with delicate veils so that nobody can see what they really look like. These robes also do a good job of hiding their bottom half, which is made of tentacles (which can be panic-inducing if you're not expecting them).

What do they want?

To allocate a lifespan to every species. Some would be allowed to go on for thousands of years, while others would be obliterated on the spot. Very harsh.

How does the Doctor know about them?

He doesn't – but he's about to!

WHO'S WHO
IN THE DARK TIMES

The Eternals

Elemental creatures who exist outside of normal time, sailing through their own realm. When they fled the Kotturuh, they gave up the chance to lead a life of their own. They rely on non-eternals, who they call Ephemerals, for entertainment. The Doctor first met a gang of Eternals when they were taking part in a solar-sailing race, which involved flying a seventeenth century pirate ship through space on solar winds. I like their style!

The Racnoss

The Racnoss are giant spiders with insatiable appetites – they are born hungry and will invade planets to feed off the locals. The Kotturuh didn't think the Racnoss were a particularly useful species, so the Racnoss went into hibernation to avoid destruction. The Empress of the Racnoss picked a cosy spot to hide out – the core of Planet Earth – and that is where the Doctor found her billions of years later.

The Osirans

This lot fled their home world and headed out across the stars, hoping to keep their race alive. They are quite full of themselves and think that they, more than anyone else, deserve the right to exist. One of them, Sutekh, did a deal with the Kotturuh for the gift of death – a bargain destined to cause the Doctor and Sarah Jane Smith a lot of trouble down the line . . .

The Great Vampires

The only race too powerful for the Kotturuh to touch. The two species came to an agreement, but the terms weren't great for the Vampires. They were allowed to keep their great power on the condition that they feed off the lives of others to remain immortal. This made them about as popular as a Weeping Angel at a wedding.

The Dæmons

Most species ran from the Kotturuh, but not the Dæmons. The Dæmons fought back and were mostly wiped out. The Kotturuh wouldn't even allow mention of the Dæmons, so they became nothing but myth. The last survivor, Azal, ended up on Earth, where he hid in suspended animation until the Master brought him back to the land of the living. That naughty Master.

The Gallifreyans

When the Kotturuh first started making their judgements, a society was evolving on Gallifrey. But they weren't yet Time Lords who could cheat death. That's another story, though . . .

THE DALEK EMPIRE

Once the Doctor got involved with the Kotturuh, things got out of control very quickly. The Daleks spotted an opportunity to exploit the situation. And with a gang of Time-Sensitive Daleks ready and waiting, they wasted no time getting stuck in. Meet the Time Squad . . .

EMERGENCY!
TIMELINE IS DIVERGING!
SITUATION MUST BE RETURNED
TO DALEK ADVANTAGE!

Time Commander

The leader of the elite Dalek Time Squad. Super-ruthless, even by Dalek standards, and determined to seize any opportunity opened up by the fluctuations in time. Fiercely loyal to the Emperor Dalek. But just how far might it be willing to go?

Strategist

This ancient Dalek has existed for a very long time and for a very good reason – it's cunning! While norma Daleks are restricted to logical thoughts, the Strategis can think the unthinkable and come up with sneaky solutions. It's seen Commanders come and go – how loyal is it to the current one?

Scientist

Works with the Strategist to come up with new and unusual plans. A whizz with temporal science, with a strong sense of how actions can affect the future – and the past! Uses time itself as a weapon, which makes this a very dangerous Dalek indeed . . .

Executioner

This guy always shoots to kill – sometimes ignoring all other orders to obliterate its victim. It's exceptionally cruel and uses pain to get results.

Drone

The basic model. Obeys orders and never thinks for itself. Or does it?

Who is Brian the Ood?

Long ago – or in the far future, depending on your point of view – the Ood were a submissive race who'd been physically altered to make them mere servants. One Ood, known as Brian, comes from that time, but he's nobody's slave. In fact, his personality is very . . . interesting.

 If you encounter Brian, take care. On one hand, he has the natural Ood instinct to be helpful and do your bidding. On the other, he's a ruthless killer. Which Brian will you get? And might you become the next victim of Mr Ball?

 One thing's for sure: Brian might have something of a split personality, but I have a soft spot for both sides . . .

DAVID SOLOMONS

OUT
NOW!

ANSWERS

PAGE 9: QUICK QUIZ ANSWER B

PAGE 11: CRACK NOOR'S CODE

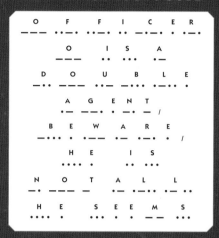

```
O   F   F   I   C   E   R
--- ..- ..- .. -.-. . .-.

    O   I   S   A
    --- .. ... .-

D   O   U   B   L   E
-.. --- ..- -... .-.. .

    A   G   E   N   T
    .- --. . -. -  /

B   E   W   A   R   E
-... . .-- .- .-. .  /

    H   E   I   S
    .... . .. ...

N   O   T   A   L   L
-. --- - .- .-.. .-..

    H   E   S   E   E   M   S
    .... . ... . . -- ...
```

PAGE 15: QUICK QUIZ ANSWER A

PAGE 21: QUICK QUIZ ANSWER B

PAGE 23: NIKOLA TESLA'S WORD SEARCH OF WONDER

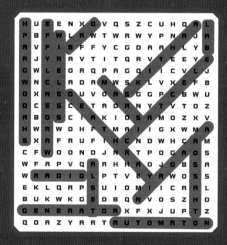

PAGE 27: QUICK QUIZ ANSWER B

PAGE 29: CATALOGUE THE CRIMINALS

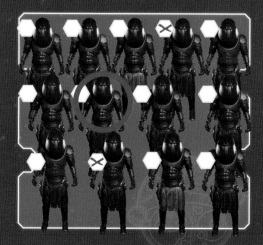

PAGE 33: QUICK QUIZ ANSWER C

PAGE 35: PRAXEUS SOURCE

START

FINISH

PAGE 39: QUICK QUIZ ANSWER A

PAGE 41: ZELLIN'S NIGHTMARE WORLD

PAGE 43: QUICK QUIZ ANSWER B

PAGE 45: MARY SHELLEY'S MONSTROUS MASH-UPS

FAM

11
1
7
16

FRIENDS

6
13
15
2

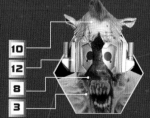

MONSTERS

10
12
8
3

VILLAINS

14
5
9
4

PAGE 49: QUICK QUIZ ANSWER A